Adaptation: Jane Brierley
Illustrations: Irina Georgeta Pusztai
Graphic design: Zapp

FAMOUS *Fables* TREASURY

5

TORMONT

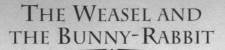

The Weasel and the Bunny-Rabbit

A little Bunny-Rabbit once lived in a large and comfortable rabbit hole.

Early one morning, when he was away searching for tender greens, along came Mrs. Weasel and settled into his home. She brought all her raggle-taggle belongings with her.

After Bunny-Rabbit had visited all the neighborhood vegetable patches, he came home to find Mrs. Weasel leaning out of one of his windows.

"Bless my tail! What have we here?" said the astonished Rabbit. "Mrs. Weasel, you'd better leave pretty fast, or I'll call all my friends and have you thrown out."

"Is that so?" said Mrs. Weasel, wiggling her pointy nose. "Things have come to a pretty pass when folks fight over a hole in the ground. What law says this hole is your property, anyway?"

"Let's ask Judge Wiley Whiskers," said the Bunny-Rabbit. "That should settle the matter."

"Fine by me," said the Weasel, who thought she knew a thing or two herself.

Now Judge Wiley Whiskers was a plump ginger Cat. He was very good at settling disputes, as we shall see.

"Come closer, my dears," he said to the Bunny-Rabbit and the Weasel. "I'm a little deaf."

As soon as they got close enough, the Cat pounced on the two animals. All of which goes to show that it is sometimes better to solve problems among ourselves.

THE MILKMAID AND HER PAIL

Once upon a time, a young Milkmaid called Perrette set off for town, carrying her milk pail balanced on her head. That morning she wore a short, plain petticoat and low-heeled shoes, so that she could walk faster.

As she followed the path, she said to herself, "I'll use the money from the milk to buy a hundred eggs. Then I'll have a hundred chickens. I'll sell the grown chickens and buy a piglet with the money. It won't cost much to fatten him with leftover vegetables. When he's good and fat, I'll sell him and buy another cow. Then I'll have twice as much milk to sell, and soon I'll be rich!"

Perrette gave a little skip at the thought of all the money she would have. Whoops! Down went the milk pail, and with it went the eggs, chickens, piglet, cow, and all the money she was dreaming about.

Poor Perrette tried her best to scoop up some of the milk, but of course it soaked into the ground. What was left was soon lapped up by the village cats.

Perrette went sadly back to the farm, thinking about all her dreams, and decided that in future she would be more careful.

"I hope you've learned your lesson," said her husband when he heard about the accident. "Never count your chickens before they're hatched!"

THE MONKEY
AND THE LEOPARD

Once upon a time a Monkey and a Leopard worked in a circus.

Each of the animals wanted to show that he could attract more visitors than the other.

The Leopard began by standing on a large drum and boasting to the audience about his good qualities.

"Ladies and gentlemen, my worth is known in the highest places," he said.

"The King himself asked to meet me. When I die, he wants my golden fur with its dazzling spots." The people loved his fur, but once they had looked at it there wasn't much else to see.

"Come here!" cried the Monkey, balancing on a large ball. "The Leopard may have golden fur and many spots, but they're only skin-deep. My mind is a wonder, and I have many clever talents."

"I can dance, do acrobatics, and perform endless tricks. You can have your money back if you're not satisfied."

The audience flocked to see the Monkey, proving that intelligence and imagination are worth more than a fine coat.

THE MONKEY AND THE CAT

Bertie the Monkey and Charlie the Cat lived in their master's house.

What a pair! They were supposed to make themselves useful, but most of the time they simply stuffed themselves with food and did as much mischief as they could.

Bertie stole things from all the neighbors. Charlie's job was to kill the mice, but he was far more interested in snatching bits of food when the Cook wasn't looking.

One day the two animals were sitting by the fire, watching some chestnuts roasting.

"Say, Brother Cat, how about pulling those chestnuts out of the fire?" said the Monkey. "Then we'll have a feast. I'd do it if I could."

The obliging Cat used his claws to pull the chestnuts out of the fire.

The Monkey scooped up all the nuts. But just then the Cook came in. "Get out!" she screamed at both the animals. The Monkey ran off, and the Cook whacked the Cat with a saucepan. And that was all the thanks the foolish Cat got for helping the sly Monkey!

THE TWO STUBBORN GOATS

When Goats are put out to pasture in the summertime, they sometimes wander high up into the rocky hills.

Two Goats had wandered off in this way, each on her own. By chance, they met on either side of a narrow wooden bridge over a rushing stream.

"Stop! I'm coming across," said the first Goat.

"Stop yourself," said the second Goat rudely. "I'm going first."

Even though Goats have a good sense of balance, these two Nanny-Goats should have trembled at the danger. Instead, each stubbornly advanced, too proud to retreat— first one step, then another, until they stood nose to nose.

"Get back!" said one.

"No, you get back!" said the other.

The two locked horns and swayed back and forth. In the struggle, they lost their balance, and both Nanny-Goats fell down,

down,

down

into the rushing, rocky stream.

Alas, pride goes before a fall!